○ ○ ○   The Bamboo Flute

The Bamboo Flute

O O O Garry Disher

TICKNOR & FIELDS
New York · 1993

Manufactured in the United States of America
Book design by David Saylor
The text of this book is set in 12 pt. Caslon 540.

BP 10 9 8 7 6 5 4 3 2

Library of Congress Cataloging-in-Publication Data

Disher, Garry.
  The bamboo flute / Garry Disher.—1st American ed.
    p.   cm.
  Summary: In a rural Australian community in 1932, twelve-year-old
Paul has his life brightened when a drifter helps him make a flute.
  ISBN 0-395-66595-7
  [1. Australia—Fiction.   2. Flute—Fiction.]   I. Title.
PZ7.D6228Bam   1993
[Fic]—dc20   92-39787   CIP   AC

To my father

〇 〇 〇　The Bamboo Flute

○ ○ ○   Chapter 1

There was once music in our lives, but I can feel it slipping away. Men are tramping the dusty roads, asking for work, a sandwich, a cup of tea. My father is bitter and my mother is sad. I have no brothers, no sisters, no after-school friends. The days are long. No one has time for music.

That's why I dream it.

I'm dreaming it now.

I'm dreaming a violin note, threading it through the quarreling cries of the dawn birds outside my window. When I do this, I do it for

Margaret, the one I love. I imagine her watching me, listening, her eyes alight.

But dreams don't last.

They're not real.

My father's boots snap on the floorboards in the hallway. The door opens. He crosses the room. For a moment the carpet strip deadens his footsteps, then his fingers tighten on my shoulder.

"Up you get, Paul."

And he's gone again. I open my eyes. The soft light of dawn is leaking through the gaps in the curtain. Five o'clock. I swing my feet onto the floor, drag on my clothes and boots, and leave the house.

My father is waiting for me at the paddock gate, his forearms on the top rail.

"Come on, son," he says.

My father is a tall man, very strong. Ever since my mother joked that he has hands "as big as frying pans," I've been fascinated by his stubby fingers and slablike palms and corded wrists. Before we got so poor, we owned a piano, but my father could never play it—each of his broad fingers would strike two keys together. I can't imagine a violin in his arms, or his fingers on the strings. When I look at his hands, I imagine them breaking things.

"Dreamer," he says. "Slowpoke."

It's not anger, when my father talks like this. It's exasperation. It's as if there is too much to do, and too little time, and I am holding him up.

He opens the gate and I follow him into the paddock. The grass is dewy this morning. Soon my boots feel lumpy and sodden.

The cows are in the farthest corner, of course. I watch my father tip back his throat and let out a whistle. It's a sharp note of frustration. These days I rarely hear his warbling whistle, the one that coils and dips like water over stones or magpies in a gum tree.

He whistles again.

Sometimes the cows respond, sometimes they don't. This time they don't, so we set out to fetch them, our boots flinging jewels of water into the eyebrow of sun on the horizon.

When we reach the cows he nods his head, sending me along their left flank, and we begin to drive them back to the milking shed. By now the sun is warming the air above the empty land. My father and I exchange shy smiles.

A rabbit streaks from the edge of the grass. It reaches a patch of red dirt pocked with burrows. There's a flash of tail, and it's gone.

Instant pandemonium.

Maddened calves charge at the fence, bulls mount the heifers, the cows kick up their heels.

"Quick," my father shouts. "Head them off, they're getting away."

He runs and I run, skirting left and right. We wave our arms and yell and caper, turning their wide-eyed, stretched-out heads, while their hooves pound like drums and a startled plover streaks up from its nest.

It doesn't take us long. They're soon calm

again. It's just high spirits, I think. The morning air feels good to them, too.

At last we bolt the rickety gate, close up the cows in the chilly shed, and begin the milking.

Milking is just one of the tasks in my endless day. After breakfast, there's a one-hour walk to school. Lessons, lunch, lessons—and rapped knuckles when I fall asleep at my desk. Then the long walk home. Chop the firewood. Collect the eggs. Weed the vegetable patch. Homework. Teatime. Bedtime.

So I dream. Who wouldn't?

I close my eyes, rest my head against the warm brown pelt of this cow, and soon I'm darting my fingers across the keys of a piano and Margaret is smiling at me with love.

"Wake up, son. Get a move on."

My father has already milked three buckets full. I have milked half a bucket. I look at his powerful fingers, watching them strip the last of the milk from the cow's teats.

Those same hands refuse to hold a gun now. Dad refuses even to own a rifle. He forbids me to play with toy guns. But when he was a soldier in Flanders' fields, did he hold a gun? Did he shoot the enemy dead?

You see, I've put two and two together. He came back from the war in 1919, married my mother, and started a family. He put the war behind him and there was music in our lives— his warbling whistle, my mother's rippling piano.

But then we got poor.

I'm twelve now and we have been poor for half of my life. He no longer whistles. The piano was sold to a man in a rattletrap truck. Music has slipped from our lives and men are tramping the roads and my father is afraid that we'll lose the farm.

It's brought the war back in his head.

O O O   Chapter 2

The cows are back in the paddock and I'm lost again, dreaming away at the kitchen table making music in my head while my porridge congeals.

A flute is leading, and now I'm drawing a piano in behind it.

But something makes me look up: my mother, making silly faces at me from across the kitchen table. She is cross-eyed, tipping her head from side to side, darting her tongue in and out.

I blush.

Her face relaxes into a smile.

"You were miles away," she says.

My father and I make her feel lonely sometimes, I think. It makes her sad. Her gift is to bring us out of ourselves.

The clock on the rickety dresser whirrs and clangs. Half-past seven. If I don't leave now, I'll be late for school again.

"Don't rush," my mother says.

But I do rush. I don't want Mr. Riggs to give me a hundred lines: *I must not be late for school.*

Five minutes later I'm half walking, half running down our potholed track to the main road. Bark snaps in the gum trees. Somewhere behind the implement shed my father starts the tractor. I hear the engine cough once or twice then catch, sending up a clatter that drives the birds from the trees.

At the front gate I pause. A man is creaking by on a bicycle, his feet on the pedals rising and falling, rising and falling, in weary revolutions. He's carrying a swag on his back, a shovel strapped to the handlebars, and he looks old and lost and tired. He's the first one I've seen on a bicycle. All the others have been on foot.

I step out onto the road. It's an hour's walk to the school. I've been doing this since Grade One—an hour there, an hour back, five days a week. How many hours is that altogether? I start to count them but the rhythm of the music takes over, filling my head again.

The wide, knobbly, dusty land is waking up. Somewhere a dog barks. A car appears from out of the north, growing larger, then passing me, tossing up grit and gravel, before diminishing on the southern horizon. A man on horseback reaches down to close a gate. Here and there, ahead of me, human figures disappear with a gulp into watery mirages—other farm kids walking to school.

The town is not very big. A grid of houses

sprawls on each side of a short main street, and there are a few trees, a garage, a playing field, and a cemetery.

Lately I have gotten into the habit of counting my way through the town to the school. It's a hundred from the culvert to the railway bridge, sixty from the bridge to the "Tarlee Slow Down" sign, eighty-five from the sign to the Post Office, and two hundred to the school boundary.

I idle along the fence line, looking in, looking for Margaret. The school is a tired-looking, one-room building trapped in buckled asphalt. The corrugated-iron roof is fringed with rust. There are only thirty town and farm kids, but at this moment there seem to be more, for they're all pushing and shoving around the water tank stand, the toilet block, the pepper trees. Besides, it's Friday—no school tomorrow—so their spirits are high.

But I can't see Margaret. Is she late again? Shall I wait out here on the road until she comes running from her house, laughing and out of breath, her braids bouncing on her shoulders? Shall I time it so that we arrive at the gate together?

Yes.

I kneel in the dust. Anyone watching me will think I'm tying my shoelaces. From this position I have a clear view of Margaret's street, the cemetery, the abandoned house on the hill.

That house. It makes me feel tight and unhappy inside. It's a secret place, but not for me— it's where Margaret and her Secret Society do secret things together.

I force myself to think about something else.

That's when I notice a movement under the gum tree opposite the school gate. A whiskery man is sitting there in the dirt, watching me, his back resting against the trunk, his forearms on his knees, a chewed stalk of grass drooping from the corner of his mouth.

Before I realize it, he has dropped his eyelid in a lazy wink.

Everything happens at once. The monitor

rings the bell, Mr. Riggs shouts at the man, "Clear out of here or I'll call the police!" and Margaret skips past me through the gate as if I don't exist.

○ ○ ○   C h a p t e r 3

Mr. Riggs hoists a rolled-up wall map onto the hook above the blackboard and lets it flap down over the date, *October 30, 1932*, chalked in blue.

"Who can tell me about The Granites?" he asks, tapping the red center of Australia with his cane.

Straight away, kids put up their hands. "Sir, sir, me sir, please sir."

I don't say anything. I look away.

Mr. Riggs lost an eye in the war, and his other eye fills me with dread. I do my best to avoid it.

Too late.

"Paul," he says. "How nice of you to be awake for a change. What can you tell me about The Granites?"

"Please, sir," I say, "granite is a hard rock."

They laugh. They always do. I arrive some mornings and find the whole school aware of things that I've missed.

Mr. Riggs taps the wall map again. He says, "The Granites, Sunshine, is an area in central Australia."

They snigger. They point at me and chant, "Sunshine!"

Mr. Riggs continues. "What is so important about The Granites?"

The roar fills the room: "GOLD."

"Gold," says Mr. Riggs. "Last week gold was found there, Paul." He smiles at me, his eye glittering, his lips a cold slash in his scarred face. "Have you noticed anything hereabouts lately?"

"Please, sir?" I say.

He is impatient.

"What happens when gold is found?"

"It's dug up, sir."

He fixes his terrible eye on me.

"Dug up," he says. "By whom?"

"Miners, sir," I say.

Mr. Riggs never supplies the answers to his questions. Instead, he asks more and more questions until we find the answers ourselves.

His next question is: "Where do they come from, these miners?" He taps the map again. "After all, Paul, The Granites are in the middle of a desert."

Is he asking me trick questions? Everyone is looking at me in secret delight, waiting for me to make more mistakes.

Guessing, I say, "Adelaide, sir."

He beams at me. "Adelaide. And many other places. Now," he says, turning back to the map, "if you were traveling from Adelaide to the goldfields, what route would you take?"

This time he looks at all of us. We look at the map. Suddenly I know the answer. But Margaret is quicker. "Please, sir," she says, "through here, through Tarlee."

Mr. Riggs nods slowly. He focuses on me again. "Paul, I'm waiting for you to put two and two together. Have you noticed anything hereabouts lately?"

Mr. Riggs was gassed in the war. He has a phlegmy voice that makes you want to cough for him. But what I am most conscious of now is the face of Margaret, the one I love: her hot cheeks, her excited eyes, her hand pressed over her cruel mouth as Mr. Riggs makes me suffer.

"Sir," I say, "lots of swaggies have been going past where I live."

"So?"

The room is still, watching me.

"I'm waiting, Paul."

His eye is gleaming like a cold flame.

"Sir," I say, "are they going to the goldfields?"

And he snaps, "What do you think?"

It isn't a proper question. I look down at my desktop, as if that will make me invisible, as if

I can disappear among the ink stains and the carved initials.

It seems to work. He forgets about me.

He says to the room, "A word of warning. There will be men who are not going to the goldfields—you saw that man hanging around the school this morning. I don't want any of you talking to strange men."

His voice croaks on and on. I begin to drift away. In my mind I am digging for gold. Gold will save us. Gold will bring back the music in our lives.

○ ○ ○   C h a p t e r   4

I pick my way through the reedy grasses at the creek's edge, a garden trowel and a biscuit tin in a wheat bag on my back. The air is warm and still, and in the buzz and snap of the insects I can sense the approach of summer. Sunlight drenches the creek bank opposite me, revealing the humped layers of the earth. Some layers are hard and red, others crumbly and black. I dream of treasures and precious metals. It's Saturday and I have hours to spare, and I have come to the creek to pan for gold.

I cry "Ho!" testing the echo.

A blazing pin prick of light on the opposite bank! A diamond?

I forge across the creek, leaping from mud to submerged stone to reedy bulrush.

But it's only a chip of flint reflecting the sun. Above, a crow slips down the air currents, calling out in mockery.

I reach the end of the path on the creek bank. The only way now is along the clifftop. As I climb up the rock face, dreaming songs, my gold-panning equipment bumps against my thigh.

At the top I rest. It is high here. I am alone, and very happy. Empty paddocks as far as the eye can see, patched together with fences and rocks and the meandering paths made by sheep.

There, where the cliff drops away, is the Old Garden.

A house was there once, late last century. Only the foundations remain, rectangles of grassy ridges on a clearing among tangled trees— quince, mulberry, apricot, fig, golden cypress, and lemon—and clumps of bamboo. I know every secret hollow and tunnel and escape route. Margaret and I could go in there and take off our clothes and no one would ever know.

The Old Garden is set back from a shallow bend where the creek has thrown up sand and pebbles. And gold, I hope.

I reach the end of the cliffs and clamber down, emerging onto coarse sand the color of rust.

And stop.

A shabby man is on the little red beach, sitting cross-legged in front of a burning log. His eyes are closed, his face tilted to the sun. I can smell fat in a frying pan. It spits. As I watch, he turns to face me. He winks, the wink I saw yesterday. He does not speak but takes a metal tube from his coat pocket. He puts it to his lips. Without taking his eyes off me, he begins to play a tune so rich and rippling it draws me to him across the sand.

He says, "Have you heard of the Pied Piper of Hamelin?"

I nod warily. I am in front of him now, next to his log fire.

"Well, I'm not him," the man says, tapping spittle from the flute.

He tucks the flute away inside his coat. It's a greatcoat, like the one my father had in the war, but this one is old, blotched with shades of black dye, and fastened with a button and three twists of wire.

And his boots—they're held together with wire, too.

He catches me looking. He winks again and says, "I forgot to polish my boots this morning."

So I try not to look at anything but his face. It's a jokey, whiskery face. His head is cocked to one side, one eyebrow raised, and his eyes and mouth are creased in a half smile. People with faces like this know what you're thinking. People like my mother.

"Sit down, Sonny Jim," he says.

Just as I settle onto the red sand, the biscuit tin clanks against the trowel in my sack. Alerted, the man says, "Running away from home?"

I stiffen. I don't know what answer to give. I don't want him to know about the gold. I don't want him to watch me, or help me. Besides, I shouldn't be talking to men like him.

Finally I mutter, "I'm picking up rubbish."

His mocking eyebrow grows even more hooked. He turns his head, looks out over the rolling paddocks and tree clumps and distant blue hills, and back at me again with his half smile. It's a way of saying: "Sonny Jim, I fail to see what sort of rubbish there'd be around here."

But he doesn't pursue the matter.

Instead he asks, "Got a name?"

"Paul."

"I'm Eric the Red," he says with a grin. "Do you believe me?"

He hasn't had a shave for some time. His whiskers are brown and white, but there is enough carroty red in them for me to reply, "I believe you."

I feel more confident now. I glance around his camp. How long has he been here? More than one day, for there are the husks of burned-out logs scattered about the place.

His tent is under a mulberry tree at the edge of the Old Garden. It's no more than an oilcloth sheet strung over a branch, its corners held down by stones. The interior is shadowy but I can see a blanket and his humped swag.

Something else makes me think he's been

here for a while: a sheep's carcass, hanging from a branch so the ants can't get to it. It has been skinned and gutted. So far, Eric the Red has cooked a leg, strips of flesh, and some chops from the rib cage. And now he's frying slices of the liver. He turns them over with a fork.

"Hungry?" he asks.

I shake my head.

"Live locally?"

I point. "Over there. You can't see it from here."

He puts his head on one side.

"The house on the main road? With the white roof?"

"Yes."

"I passed it yesterday," says Eric the Red, "when I went into town."

He gestures with his hand. "These trees and paddocks and the creek—are they all part of your farm?"

"Yes."

He is watching me as if he wants to laugh. He

says, "I don't think your dad would like it if he knew I was camped here."

I like Eric the Red, so my first impulse is to say we don't mind. Then I remember my father's fury when men come to the back door wanting tea, a sandwich, a job. So I don't say anything.

"He wouldn't, would he?" laughs Eric the Red, looking into my head.

I shift uncomfortably. I look away. Then Eric the Red says, "Do you like music?"

I look back at him. "Yes."

"Play anything?"

"I was going to learn the piano but we had to sell it."

Margaret's mother teaches piano. When I find gold, I will buy us another piano and pay for my lessons and learn what Margaret and the other kids do, find out where they go after school every day.

But I can't tell Eric the Red these things.

"Ever played a flute?" he asks.

"No."

He fetches his flute from inside his coat pocket and begins to play it, running notes up and down the scale. "Here, try," he says, offering it to me.

The metal has been warmed by his body. That makes me feel strange. The bumps and scratches of his hard life are all over it. I want him to look away so I can wipe where his mouth has been. And I don't know where to put my fingers. My elbows are stuck out—I must look like our goose flying at the sheepdog.

Eric the Red says, half smiling again, "Wipe it if you like."

So I don't.

He gets up and sits beside me. His skin smells of the sun, his clothes of wood smoke.

"Like this," he says, twisting my fingers and arms this way and that. "Now, blow. Across the hole, not into it."

I produce a sound like the fluffing snores of a grandfather in an armchair.

"Try again,' says Eric the Red. "tilt it a bit."

A note? Weak and wobbly, but still a proper note.

"Now lift one finger at a time."

More notes, each one different.

"See?" says Eric the Red. "Easy. The hard part is the next ten years of practice."

I must look downhearted, for he says, "But you might be a natural. Who knows?"

I want a flute. Its sweet tone pulls at my feelings. I can hear flutes in the songs I dream.

Reluctantly I pass Eric the Red his flute. "I haven't got any money," I tell him.

He understands. "Why don't you make yourself one?"

I think of the rubbish behind our shearing shed, the scraps of pipe and wire and angle iron. "Every piece is precious," my father always tells me.

So I ask Eric the Red, "How do you make a flute?"

He inclines his head toward a corner of the Old Garden. "See over there?"

He's indicating a stand of bamboo stalks clumped together like quarreling, tattered feather dusters. "Perfect for flutes," he says.

He smiles, raises his flute, and "Danny Boy" spreads and rises around me.

Chapter 6

My father's toolshed resembles a dim, warm, blurry cave. I like to search its dark corners for his boxes of useful, unused gadgets, or study the wasps in the gappy split-log walls. Soft puffs of dust cover the tools and the benches. Dust motes blaze in the bands of sunlight.

I am drilling holes. This piece of bamboo, cut for me by Eric the Red yesterday, is smooth and round and the color of honey. I have already drilled two holes in the shaft. Now I'm drilling the third, exactly where Eric the Red nicked it with his pocketknife.

I wonder if he's still at the Old Garden. When we said good-bye yesterday he said, looking at my sack, "Sure you're not running away?"

I was embarrassed, and muttered, "I'm looking for gold."

But he didn't laugh, or suddenly look greedy. "This isn't gold-bearing country," he said.

I asked him if he was going to The Granites.

He had rolled his eyes and laughed. "Heat? Flies? Hard work? And look at the state of my boots!"

I didn't look. We shook hands and I walked home before it got too late.

Sunday today. School tomorrow. I should be doing homework. But I want to finish the flute. I've been thinking of nothing else.

It's not easy. I've wrapped the shaft in my handkerchief to protect it from the jaws of the vise, but the drill bit churns and tears no matter how gently I turn the handle.

A voice outside: "Paul? Where are you? Paul!"

My father. He's coming in here. I have an image of his big hands.

I scoop the tube out of the vise, tuck it into my pants, blow away the shavings. "Coming, Dad."

The door opens. "What are you doing? Mum needs wood for the fire."

That's how he speaks these days. His face is always clenched with the cares of the world, he's never still, everything is work, work, work.

"Just mucking around, Dad."

"Time for that later."

When I was a little kid, Sundays were slow days of quietness and best clothes and church and no work. Now our best clothes are worn out, and we can't afford gas, and there's always work to do, and my father says observing the Lord's day does you no good at all.

I follow him out of the shed. The flute starts to slip. I can feel it edging down inside my pants. I clamp my hands in my pockets to stop it. This makes me walk as though I'm drunk.

My father pauses, looks at me oddly, shakes his head. "You're a funny kid sometimes," he says. "Come on, Dreamer, get a move on."

I walk toward the house, he toward the sheds. At the tank stand I stop, quickly sliding the flute into a secret place. Out of habit, I rap my knuckles against the tank. The water level is low. It's always low. Then I trail my fingers over the calcified deposit left by years of seepage from a tiny hole at the base of the tank. It's lumpy, hard, and wet. On hot days I like to lick it.

The wood heap is beside the back fence. Chopping wood is the job I hate most. I hate the iron-hard logs, the twisting axe handle, the chips and the splinters and the gliding snakes in summer.

It helps if I turn it into music. *Chop* two three four, *chop* two three four. Or a waltz: *chop* two three, *chop* two three.

I am doing this when I hear the *brrrup brrrup* of Toby's hooves. My father, cantering across the yard and into the lane out of sight. This is one

of his Sunday jobs. He patrols the fences, checks
the dams, scouts for troubled ewes and cows.

Suddenly I feel afraid. Two things are clear to
me. When my father crosses the creek at the Old
Garden, he will come upon Eric the Red. And
the butchered sheep in the mulberry tree was
ours, not Eric the Red's.

I'll get into trouble, *chop* into trouble, *chop* . . .
chop . . . *chop*.

○ ○ ○   Chapter 7

I can't stay out here forever. With a stack of
prickly logs in my arms, I return to the house,
to the wood box by the kitchen stove.

My mother smiles. "Thank you, dear."

The room smells of fresh paint. The wooden
table and three of its chairs stand yellow and
gleaming on sheets of newspaper, and my mother
is kneeling with a dripping brush at the fourth
chair. She's wanted to do this for weeks. She
kept saying, "The kitchen needs brightening."
I think she really meant our lives needed
brightening.

Then last Tuesday she walked to town with a basket of eggs and came back with a rusty, dented tin of old paint.

I begin to stack the firewood in the box. Behind me, my mother is humming, her paintbrush gently slapping the chair.

Just being in a room with her calms me down.

"Mum," I say, "I'm making a flute."

"A flute?"

"Out of bamboo."

She sits back on her heels. Paint runs down the handle and over her hand, but she doesn't seem to notice it. She treats the things I say seriously. She doesn't think I'm strange. She says, "Do you know where to put the finger holes?"

I nod. "Someone showed me."

"Bamboo, eh? Where did you get the bamboo?"

"The Old Garden."

She smiles. "I remember. I haven't been down there for years."

I wait for a while, then I ask, "Mum, what would you do if you knew someone was living at the Old Garden?"

She never wastes time, my mother. She narrows her eyes at me and says, "Paul, what did you see?"

Eric the Red is my secret. But my mother's clever eyes are looking into my head. I'll have to say something. "I found an old camp fire."

My mother isn't satisfied, but she doesn't question me any further. Instead, she returns to her painting, saying, "Don't tell your father about it. He's got enough worries."

At this very minute, is my father cracking his stock whip over the head of Eric the Red? I shiver. "Mum," I say, "can you teach me to play the flute?"

She murmurs, "I'll certainly try." She doesn't look at me. She's busy with a tricky part on the chair rungs.

Then we hear tuneless whistling outside, and footsteps on the back veranda.

"Put the kettle on, dear," my mother says.

"Pardon?"

Patiently she says, "Put the kettle on."

The kettle is always full, resting on the edge of the stove. It grumbles as soon as I set it down on the hot iron slab. At the same moment, there's a knock on the door.

"Ask what he wants, dear," my mother says, still concentrating on the chair.

The man at the back door is small and apologetic like a nervous dog. But when he sees I'm a kid his face grows cunning.

"By yourself?" he asks.

I open my mouth to reply, but my mother's voice calls sharply and clearly, "Paul, ask him what he wants."

"My mother says what do you want."

The man tries to look over my shoulder. "Is your dad home?"

I've got my wits about me now. "Yes."

"Ah. Well, tell your mum I'm a bit thirsty and peckish."

As if remembering his manners, he takes off his hat and runs the brim between his fingers. It's an old hat, greasy and dusty. Everything about him is greasy and dusty.

"Tell him," calls my mother, "you'll bring him out a jam sandwich and a cup of tea."

The man nods many times and backs off the porch. "Good-oh," he says. "Ta. Much obliged. I'll just wait out here, shall I?"

He is nothing like Eric the Red.

I return to the kitchen. The kettle lid is clupping up and down. My mother says, "There's a loaf in the crock. Cut two slices, and use the apricot jam. One pinch of tea in the pot will be enough."

She returns to her painting and I make the sandwich and let the tea brew in the pot. "What cup?" I ask.

"He'll have a cup of his own, if he's got any sense."

I carry the sandwich, the teapot, and the sugar bowl across the kitchen and out the back door.

The swaggie gets up from the veranda step. "Ta," he says.

"You have to use your own cup," I tell him.

"Right you are." He rummages in his swag, finds a chipped enamel mug, and holds it out. I pour the tea and let him spoon the sugar: one, two three, four, five. How can he drink it so sweet? And I want to tell him, "We're not made of money."

"Lovely," he says, taking a bite from his sandwich and washing it down with tea.

I watch him curiously. "Are you going to The Granites?"

"Bloody oath I am," he says.

It's at that point that I see my father riding Toby hard and fast across the paddocks. "Quick," I tell the man. "You have to go. My father doesn't like swaggies."

"Christ Almighty," the man says.

He gulps down the tea, tosses out the dregs, stuffs the rest of the sandwich in his pocket, and runs.

Eric the Red would never run.

I take the teapot and sugar bowl back into the kitchen. "Dad's back," I say.

My mother stiffens. "Did he see the swaggie?"

"Don't think so."

"Thank God for that," she says. She is very relieved. Three or four men come in off the road every day, and she never turns them away, but she feels the strain of my father's disapproval.

We wait then, tense and silent. I can feel the beating of my heart. My mother's paintbrush slides up and down on the same spot.

Then the eruption. The back door slams, his boots pound down the hallway, and my father is standing huge with anger in the kitchen doorway.

"Thieving mongrels!" he explodes. "I've had enough."

My mother wipes her brush on the lip of the paint tin, replaces the lid, and gets to her feet.

"Calm down and tell us what's wrong."

"Calm down? They're butchering our sheep left, right, and center." He turns to look at me. "You were down there yesterday. See anyone?"

"Down where?" my mother says.

"The Old Garden," my father says.

Suddenly he seems weary. He sighs and pushes his hat to the back of is head. "Someone's been camping there. He butchered a perfectly good ewe."

"I expect he was hungry," my mother says.

"Then why doesn't he bum a sandwich off you like all the other no-hopers?" Again he looks at me. "I asked you if you saw anyone yesterday."

I like to tell myself it's not a lie if you tell part of the truth. So I say to my father, "I saw where someone made a camp fire."

"What about the dead sheep?"

"I was just passing," I tell him.

"Well, you should have told me. Whoever was camped there is long gone by now."

My father is tight like a spring. He turns to leave the room.

My mother tugs on his sleeve. "You're not going to do anything silly, are you?"

He faces her again. "Silly? I'm reporting this to the police. Tell me what's silly about that."

We hear him stride away from the house. A little later, Toby's hooves begin their drumming on the hard ground. My mother turns to me, touches me, and says softly, "Paul, you'd better tell me who you met down there."

O O O   C h a p t e r 8

Monday morning. We are lined up in the school-
yard, big kids at the front, down to little kids at
the back. I feel tired—from the milking and the
long walk to school—and tense because my father was so tense in the paddock, in the milking
shed, at breakfast. I could easily fall asleep on
my feet. But we're reciting with Mr. Riggs, sa-
luting the flag, honoring the King and the Em-
pire. Then we march into school: *left, left, left
right left*, one kid beating the drum, another the
triangle. And I think: this would sound much
better with a flute.

I have spent seven years in this room. I have moved across it from left to right, from the Grade Ones to the Grade Sevens, and never once in a desk at the back. It's because I fall asleep, or watch the world outside the window, making songs in my head. Every year I'm told the same thing. "I want you where I can keep an eye on you, Sunshine."

Sunshine. They always laugh. I'm even called Sunshine by the stationmaster and the baker.

While the little kids are walking in and Mr. Riggs isn't looking, I take the flute from my knapsack and hide it in my desk.

Was I seen? Something is going on at the back of the room. Lots of giggling and whispering among the town kids. Something about Margaret. She catches me looking at her and immediately pokes out her tongue, and they all cluster and laugh and hide their desirable life from me.

"Good morning, Paul."

I jump in fright. I turn to face the front. Mr. Riggs then says, "Good morning, school."

"Good morning, Mr. Riggs," we chant, like words in a prayer.

"Be seated."

And we sit. The same thing every day. Seven years of it.

The room never changes. It smells of chalk dust and dirty pants and kids from families who never wash. The initials AG, carved in my desktop, belong to Arthur Goss, Margaret's father, so badly wounded in the war that no one has ever seen him. Every desk bears years of scars and ink stains. There are wall maps, colored drawings marked ten out of ten, numbers zero to twelve, letters A to Z, dusty crossed flags above a vanished wall plaque naming the war dead, seven rows of kids, and, at the front, Mr. Riggs and his desk, the big blackboard behind him.

The morning drags by. The little kids practice the alphabet, the middle kids do dictation, Grade Sevens do arithmetic. Then recess.

Now we're doing adverbs and adjectives.

Another thing about Mr. Riggs: he is missing the fingers of his left hand. His habit is to hook one end of his cane into the stub of flesh, the other end into his good palm, and push inward.

Stillness settles us when he does that. We sit, watching the cane bow and straighten, bow and straighten, then *whap!*—he slams the blackboard, and we all jump and look down at our work.

Adverbs and adjectives.

I am lost in words: walking *hurriedly;* talking *unhappily; stormy* sea; *crumbling* rock.

Then Mr. Riggs says, "Have you finished, Margaret Goss?"

We all look up. Behind me, Margaret says, "Sorry, sir," and we all return to our work.

The minutes pass. More scrapes and whispers at the back of the room. Then the crack of the cane.

"*Margaret.* If it's so interesting, perhaps you would like to share it with the whole school?"

Margaret *never* gets told off. I feel half pleased and half sorry.

"Please, sir," says her friend Joy Bailey, the policeman's kid, "it was Margaret's birthday on the weekend."

"Was it, indeed? How old are you, Margaret?"

"Please, sir, twelve, sir."

"Did you have a party?"

There is another stir of giggling, of feet shuffling on the floor.

"Yes, sir."

A party. I feel hot inside. What did they do? Where did they go? Did they take their clothes off?

"Back to work," Mr. Riggs says. "All of you."

I look down at my workbook. I can't write anything.

I've got pictures in my head: the kids at the party, waiting for the mothers to go away, then racing down the broad, slow streets, past the dusty gum trees whose bark peels and branches crack on hot days, to places only they know about. Places where no one can see them. They dare each other: who will do it first? If Margaret is ever dared, she will do it, she's not afraid. I can see her bright eyes and her hot face and her skin.

I don't realize it, but I'm humming, and it's a jumpy, out-of-breath tune.

I wake up to all their terrible laughter. Mr. Riggs's eye is glittering at me like broken glass.

But, "It's lunchtime," is all he says.

We march out in orderly lines. Fresh air. We scatter to the ends of the yard.

I always sit under the pepper trees with other farm kids. Lunch today is an apricot jam sandwich. Sometimes my mother packs a bun too, but not today. Lately she's been trading all our eggs.

The trouble with the farm kids is that all they talk about is engines and bags-per-acre. The trouble with the town kids is that they have secrets and no place for me. I sit, with my back against a tree trunk, looking across the yard at the town beyond the school fence, and the flat empty land, and the long road stretching north and south.

Did Margaret take them to the abandoned house? Did they go there after her party? No one would disturb them there.

Then we play cricket until the bell rings. I'm always sent out to the boundary. They say I don't concentrate enough to be near the batsmen. They say I'd forget my head if it wasn't screwed on.

I like it here on the boundary. Just now two men are squeaking by on bicycles, loaded down with bags and shovels and boxes tied with string. Off to The Granites? And here's a Ford truck, two men in the front, two in the back. They wave. I wave.

That's why I don't notice the cricket ball bounce past me and hit the fence. Four runs to the batsman. There are jeers and shouts and calls for my death.

I close my mind to them and think of the flute.

During the first lesson after lunch, unhappiness overcomes me and I take the flute out of my desk and hold it in my lap, hunched over the desk so that I can't be seen. The smooth shaft brings me comfort. I stroke it with my fingertips and let my thumbpad rest in the three burry finger holes. Tonight, tomorrow night—I'll soon finish making it, soon be playing it.

Am I humming again? A shadow falls across my workbook. Mr. Riggs says, "Bring it out, Sunshine."

"Sir?"

"Whatever you're playing with. Bring it out and put it on the desk."

"It's nothing, sir."

"I don't care if it's the crown jewels. Bring it out."

I cannot look at Mr. Riggs, at that scarred face lit by that eye. I place the flute gently in the desktop groove with my pen and pencils. I return my hand to my lap. My movements are so slight, so inoffensive, surely I'm invisible?

He picks up the flute. "Now get on with your work," he says. He raises his voice to take in the room: "All of you."

He's not interested in what I've been making. He doesn't even examine it. The last I see of that flute is a honeyed flash of bamboo as he throws it in the rubbish bin.

The whole district is gripped by the exploits of Eric the Red.

Tuesday, Wednesday, Thursday: I hear a new story every day. He has killed and eaten hundreds of sheep, dozens of cows, thousands of hens. He has stolen truckloads of eggs and whole wardrobes of clothing, and burgled every house around. He's a radical, a war hero, a bandit, a black-sheep English lord. His hair is black, red, straight, curly. He's five feet ten inches tall one day and six feet six inches tall the next. He's been seen on every back road to the north, south, east, and west of us; he's even been seen in town. Constable Bailey says he'll question him; the farmers say they would like to shoot him.

Eric the Red has been a bad and busy man.

I don't say anything to anyone about him. I work on my new flute.

After Monday's loss I raced through my chores, hurried to the Old Garden with a hand-saw, and was back with another bamboo piece before dinner, dishes, homework, and bed. On Tuesday I drilled the first holes. Yesterday I drilled the remaining holes. No one knows. I hide the tube in my knapsack at school and in the water tank stand at home.

And now it's Thursday after school and I'm in the toolshed, smoothing the chipped edges with sandpaper.

Scrape, scrape: it makes my skin creep, like fingernails on a blackboard.

I'm safe for the next hour. My father has gone

to Adelaide in his fraying suit and won't be back before six.

Scrape, scrape. I can't do any more. Surely it's finished now.

I unclamp the flute from the jaws of the vise, blow away the dust, put it to my lips.

The angle must be wrong. All I get is a hoarse rush of air. I twist the shaft slightly, turning the rim away from my bottom lip, and blow again.

A sound so soft and clear, I want to soar to the roof.

Now I place my fingers over the holes in the shaft and blow again, tapping each fingertip up and down. The notes emerge like the songs of raucous birds far away, but there is music there if I have the patience to find it.

I run across to the house. I fling open the kitchen door.

"Mum? Listen!"

She is sitting on a yellow chair at the yellow table, sewing patches inside the knees of old trousers. She looks up, smiling, her eyes bright.

Standing as if I'm as light as air, I crook my elbows, take a breath, and blow.

Wobbly sounds, with watery hesitations at the ends of them.

"Wait, wait," I say.

I try again. My fingertips, my breathing is steady, and this time the notes float softly into the air between us.

She claps her hands. "Bravo!"

Some things are better than all the gold in the ground. There's no stopping me now. As I play, my mother listens, turned toward me, assessing each note.

Then she puts down her mending and joins me. "Try putting one, two, and three different fingers up and down together, in different combinations," she says.

Soon tunes are emerging. "Jingle Bells." "God Save the King." I could go on all night. The kitchen clock ticks from five o'clock to six o'clock. We fill the kitchen with song.

Later she says, looking at me quizzically, "Did you learn to play these songs at school?"

That's a laugh. One loose-skinned drum, one clangy triangle, thirty out-of-tune voices. "We don't have music at school."

"That's what I thought,' she says. She is still looking at me in that odd way. "Do you know what I think? I think you can play by ear."

I don't know what she means by that.

"It means," she explains, "that once you have heard a tune you can play it without having to read the music."

Play by ear. I feel that I could lead a pipe-and-drum band across the curve of the earth.

"Are you going to show Dad?" she asks.

I shrug and shift about nervously. What if he breaks it? What if he says, "There's no time for all this tomfoolery?" His words, his tone, sound clear in my mind.

"Go on," my mother says. "He'll be proud of you, I know he will."

But if I show my father the flute, must I also tell him about Eric the Red?

My mother reads my worried thoughts. She says, "Eric the Red will be our secret. What matters is that you've made a beautiful flute and you play it beautifully."

I'm about to thank her with "Danny Boy" when we hear a storming shout outside, full of bitter hate and rage. "Mongrel! Clear off before I slit your throat."

I jump. "Dad's home."

This is stating the obvious. My mother looks at me, tired, patient, gathering the energy to turn his wrath.

I hide the flute in my sleeve, and my mother, noticing, nods regretfully. "Later," she murmurs.

Then he's in the kitchen. He seems to fill it. "I just chased off one of your *friends*," he snarls. "He won't be back in a hurry."

He glowers at us.

I can sense something else there, underneath. He's been to see the man at the bank and returned with empty hands. We're poor and we'll stay poor until the luck turns. The last thing my father wants this evening is a clever son with a golden flute and a song.

○ ○ ○   C h a p t e r   1 0

Friday. The last lesson of the week. I'm plotting
the routes of the explorers in my workbook. The
flute is in the knapsack at my feet. It has been
there all day, hidden, but so alive in my thoughts
that I seem to be attached to it with invisible
strings.

"Pens down," Mr. Riggs says.

He must be in pain today. His face looks
clammy and pale.

"Children," he says, "before you pack up to
go, Constable Bailey would like to say a few
words."

We look toward the classroom door. I don't know how long Constable Bailey has been standing there. He is a puffy-faced man with hair streaked like oily string across his balding scalp. When he walks his shoes squeak. He smiles into the room, showing his yellow teeth. He's been here once before, wanting to know who kept jamming potatoes up the mail truck's exhaust pipe. No one owned up then; no one will own up now.

"Children," he says, wagging his uniform cap on his forefinger, "as you know, there's been a lot of stealing going on late."

Mr. Riggs interrupts: "Mr Bailey is not blaming *you*," he says.

The constable laughs. "That's right. No one's blaming you. The trouble's coming from outsiders."

He's beaming at everyone. But I'm not fooled for a minute. I'm the one he's really after. He wants me to tell on Eric the Red.

"We've had reports," he continues, "of chickens and sheep being killed and eaten, food stolen from people's houses, gates left open, fences down, fires lit."

He pauses. He looks at Mr. Riggs, and I can sense that what he's going to say next is making him embarrassed.

"Strange men have been seen lurking in the district," he says. "Now I want you to promise me you'll have nothing to do with these men. You know the golden rule: never talk to strangers."

For a moment, Constable Bailey's gaze lingers on me. I feel my face redden. He looks away. "One man in particular. He wears an old black coat and he's got a red beard. If you see this man, or anyone acting suspiciously, keep away from him and tell me, or Mr. Riggs, or your parents. Any questions?"

All at once, half the school has a question, kids shooting up their hands, going, "Ooh ooh, please sir, me sir," calling Constable Bailey "sir" like he's a teacher.

"Goodness me," he says. He's enjoying him-self. He answers all the idiotic questions about crimes you'd need a whole army of thieves for, not one man by himself. All the kids have seen something or someone. And they're all bright-eyed, imagining danger, imagining how they'll arrest Eric the Red themselves.

"Hold on," Constable Bailey says, laughing, holding up both hands. "Just remember: if you see anything, report it; don't try to be heroes."

Then he shakes hands with Mr. Riggs's stump and says good-bye. When he's gone, Mr. Riggs stands watching us. "When you're ready," he says.

One by one we settle down. When we're standing at attention, he says, "Good afternoon, everybody."

"Good afternoon, Mr. Riggs."

Our words go up and down like a stupid song in need of a breezy tune on my flute.

Just as we are filing out, Mr. Riggs stops me.

"Paul, I want you to stay behind for a minute, please."

I thought so. They all know about me and Eric the Red. Constable Bailey is probably waiting outside, or Mr. Riggs is going to drag me off to the police station himself. All the kids snigger as they pass me. Margaret grins. Joy grins.

When they're all gone, Mr. Riggs says, "I want you to explain this, Paul."

He's holding a length of bamboo—the confiscated, unfinished flute.

I look up. There is kindness in his face. It transforms his terrible eye. I feel confused.

"Sir, I was making a flute, sir."

He nods. "I can see that." He offers it to me. "You'd better take it home and finish it."

I take it from him. For a while, neither of us speaks. I gather myself and look at his eye and say, "Sir, I made another one."

An expression of regret passes over his face. "Did you? I would have given this one back to you, but I thought it was just a stick. When I was burning the rubbish yesterday, I realized what it was."

"That's all right, sir."

We stand there, feeling awkward.

He looks at me curiously. "Can you play?"

"Yes, sir."

"Then you must show me on Monday."

Another one of those long pauses. "Sir," I say, "I can show you now. I've got the other one in my knapsack.

He folds his arms and leans against the edge of his desk and says, "All right then, let's hear you."

I take out the flute, my fingers fluttery in the gaze of his shiny eye. Then I position myself and begin to play, and the magic takes over.

He's smiling.

Mr. Riggs is listening and smiling.

I finish, feeling hot-faced and shy.

Mr. Riggs says, "That's made my day."

Then he looks at me thoughtfully. "The

school concert is in a few weeks. Think you can play something for us?"

I flash my answer. "Yes, sir."

"Good."

He stands upright, brushing chalk dust from his hands. He's returning to his briskness and severity, so I pick up my knapsack to go.

"Good-bye, sir."

He nods, nothing more, busy again with something on his desk.

The thing is, I feel too excited and happy to go home yet. I want the world to know of my triumph. I want Margaret to know.

I stop for a while at the school gate. I should turn left, I should walk the long miles home, through the shimmering mirages that disappear before I ever reach them.

Instead, I turn right, down the main street, making for the northern edge of town. There's a lot going on: mothers and fathers and kids doing shopping for the weekend, miners traveling north to The Granites.

Beyond the last house it's farmland again. The cemetery is set among gum trees at the top of a sloping paddock. A short distance downhill from it is the abandoned house.

I climb through the twanging fence wires and cut across the paddock. The closer I get to the house, the more it resembles a broad, waiting face. The windows are the eyes; the door is the nose; the crumbling step, the teeth; the rusty roof, the fringe of hair.

I realize why it's so ideal as the town kids' secret place. They would spot the approach of anyone in plenty of time to escape or cover up what they're doing.

I get closer and closer. There's no sign of life in the house. Margaret and the others must have seen me by now. I hope they don't run out the back way. I want them to hear me play.

Instead of going in, I circle the house. The grimy insect screens are torn and bulging. The chimney and one wall show signs of weather damage. Weeds choke the garden beds. The pitted roof is beginning to fall in. The back door is open and almost off its hinges.

I call out: "Anyone there?"

No answer. I step closer and peer in.

It's clear to me that this is their entrance. Feet have worn a path up to the door, and I can see footprints on the dusty linoleum inside.

I go in. "Hello? Anyone here?"

My answer comes at once—"Danny Boy" piped mournful and low from somewhere toward the front of the house.

I find Eric the Red sitting in a corner of one of the front rooms, his back against the wall. Next to him are an unrolled blanket, his swag, and a tin plate of cold cooked chops. He doesn't interrupt his playing, but watches me enter, cross the room, and settle on the floor opposite him.

"Paul," he says.

I feel too agitated to say hello. I say, "Everyone's after you."

He nods, "Yes, I expect they are."

"My father wants to slit your throat."

He smiles and nods again.

I watch his unconcerned face. I ask, "Did you really do all those things?"

He gives me one of his looks.

"Got myself a reputation, have I?"

"Everyone's after you."

"It wouldn't be the first time," he says, "and it won't be the last."

I realize now what happens to men like Eric the Red: when they do a little thing wrong, they get blamed for all the crimes and mistakes in the universe. He scratches his red whiskers. He doesn't seem to care. He should be more worried.

I say, "Today the policeman told us we have to look out for you. We're not allowed to talk to you."

"You're talking to me," he says with a grin.

I feel confused. We sit there—me troubled, Eric the Red placidly smiling. Then I remember. "I made the flute!"

This wakes him up. His voice booms: "Good for you!"

"Took me ages."

"Ah, but can you play anything?"

I take the flute from my knapsack. I position myself, take a breath, and begin to play.

The notes sound weak in here. And I must be nervous, for they fade at the ends like someone lowering his voice.

Eric the Red holds out his hand. "Let me try."

He fits himself comfortably to my flute, his fingers tap, and "Danny Boy" leaks sadly into the dim, dusty room.

He stops playing and looks critically at my handiwork. "The holes should be bigger," he says, "and better shaped."

He folds out the blade of his pocketknife. It winks in the late afternoon light from the window. If Constable Bailey and Mr. Riggs and all the others saw this now, they would shout at me, "Paul, watch out!"

I feel no fear.

I watch as Eric the Red gently, deftly, shaves the edges of the finger holes in my flute.

"Now," he says, putting it to his lips again. The sound is smoother and richer this time, better than in my father's toolshed, better than in the kitchen at home. How could I have believed that the flute was finished?

"Position comes into it," says Eric the Red. He returns the flute, pushes and pulls at my wrists and fingers, shows me how to angle my lips.

"And you mustn't blow too jerkily."

When he's satisfied, he draws up his knees and rests his forearms on them. "Well, Paul, are you going to arrest me?"

He's making me feel strange, talking like this. I get up and cross to the window. At first all I can see is the town, the road, and a solitary car glinting briefly in the sinking rays of the sun. It's getting late. Clouds are gathering. I'd better go home.

Suddenly I feel myself stiffen in alarm. There

is a deceptive hollow in the lower reaches of the paddock, and I can see heads appearing, then shoulders, trunks, and legs.

Margaret striding, braids bouncing, her tartan skirt swirling about her knees, followed by Roger, Colin, Stanley, and Joy.

I jerk back from the window. "Some kids are coming. One of them's the policeman's kid. You have to go."

He sighs. "My weary bones." With difficulty, he stands up, all his joints creaking, and joins me at the window. The kids are quite close now. In two or three minutes they'll be here.

"Quick," I tell him. "You have to get away."

But Eric the Red stands right in the middle of the window, as if he's inviting discovery. Doesn't he care? He leans forward, peering. "Can they run fast? Do you reckon I could beat them?"

I can't bear this. I can't keep still. I push him on the shoulder. "Please. You'll get caught."

At last he turns away from the window. He

returns to the corner, folds and straps his swag together, and hoists it up on his shoulder.

Then I realize he's offering something to me. "I want you to have this," he says. "A gift."

I turn it over in my hands. It's a letter opener, a strip of beaten brass in the shape of a wavy-bladed knife. Coiling patterns have been etched along the rippling blade.

"I made it in the war," he says, "when things were quiet in the trenches. We all did it."

I follow him through the house, imagining the mud and the thundering guns. The war is a thread running through too many lives. But Eric the Red is whistling as if he's never been to war, whistling "What Shall We Do with the Drunken Sailor?" as if he's got all the time in the world.

And then he's through the door and into the trees around the cemetery and gone.

But he still might be seen.

I know what I'll do: I'll distract them.

Leaving my knapsack by the back door, I march along the side of the house and then down the slope toward the town, playing the flute as I go. The air is still. My music trembles, gathering strength, rolling along like smoke before me.

It stops the town kids in their tracks.

Then Margaret says, beginning to smile at me shyly, "Do you want to come with us? Don't go home yet."

○ ○ ○   C h a p t e r   1 2

My father is going on and on: "Never come home late like that again. You had us both very worried. We didn't know where you were."

I mumble, "Sorry."

I'm hunched over my cold, stiff pudding. They have finished eating dinner—"hours ago," as he keeps telling me.

It's a night of storm clouds and no moon. The window is black where the curtains fail to meet. My mother is entering figures in the farm ledger. *Scratch*, *scratch*, goes her fountain-pen nib. My father is standing with his back to the stove and his hands on his hips, looking at me hard. He says, "Anything can happen. You've heard the stories going around."

I clatter down my knife and fork and look at him and say, "He wouldn't hurt anyone."

"Who wouldn't?" he demands.

I have nearly trapped myself as usual. I quickly shrug and say, "The man they keep talking about."

"Man?" scoffs my father. "A hundred men. A thousand. More every day. Every one of them a ratbag. Or worse."

I let him go on. He'll wind down soon.

It's warm in here, comfortable with cooking smells and my mother's quiet presence. My head is full of thoughts and song. I don't remember the long walk home in darkness, only Margaret in the abandoned house, the thrilling secret rituals, my vow of eternal silence.

"What were you doing in town anyway?" my father says. "What kept you? Who were you playing with?"

Suddenly I realize the best way to handle this, the best way to shift him to a different topic. I look across at my mother, and then up at him, and I tell him: "I was showing Mr. Riggs my flute."

He frowns. "Your flute?"

"I'm going to play it in the school concert."

He is looking puzzled. But my mother smiles, caps her fountain pen, and claps her hands together. "Paul, that's wonderful."

"Did you buy him a flute? You know we can't afford a flute."

"He made it," my mother says proudly.

My father looks from one of us to the other. He's not sure how to respond. Part of him wants to show his usual disapproval, but he's also curious, and my mother's delight is thawing him a little.

He pulls out a yellow chair and sits, his arms folded. "Let's see it, then," he says, as if he only half believes us.

I push away my dirty dessert plate and fetch

the knapsack. My father watches as I tumble everything onto the kitchen table: lunch box; Eric the Red's letter opener; books; colored pencils; a limp, leaking brown banana; the bamboo flute.

I pass him the flute. I watch his hands. They are clumsy hands unused to beauty, hands that don't know their own strength.

Troubled, I look up at his face. As I watch him, the severe lines fade a little from his eyes and mouth. He seems to struggle. Finally he says, "Very good."

Before I can stop myself I say, "I had some help with it."

"From Mr. Riggs?"

I can't say yes. What if he talks to Mr. Riggs about it? I open and close my lips without speaking.

"Son?" my father says. "Who helped you?"

I look in panic at my mother. She says, "It's all right, Paul."

So I say, "Eric the Red."

"Who's he when he's at home?"

My father's jaw is jutting out. He wants to get to the bottom of this. Just then, my mother reaches out her hand and touches his forearm. "Someone Paul met on the road. There's nothing to worry about."

One expression follows another on my father's face. He is suspicious, worried, and regretful that we have to hide things from him.

Then he folds his arms and looks at the wall. "All right, let's hear you play something."

I pick up the flute. My body seems to sway in anticipation. I shape myself to the little piece of bamboo and begin to play. I don't miss a note.

I watch him. First he nods, then, despite himself, he turns to watch me, a slow smile starting across his face.

When I finish, he says, shaking his head, "I had no idea. I had no idea."

I think it's a compliment.

I move on to "Greensleeves"—but I play no

more than a couple of bars when I notice that he's become rigid. He's staring intently at the junk from my knapsack.

The letter opener.

He pounces on it. "Did you make this, too?"

I can't tell what he's feeling. The expression in his eyes is too complicated. I don't know if I should be afraid or not. Then he says softly, "It's years since I saw one of these."

Abruptly he puts it down, pushes back his chair, and leaves the room.

He returns with an old hatbox. He takes off the lid. "There was a time when I made things, too, you know."

We watch him unpack the box. There are five parcels, each wrapped untidily in old newspapers. I lean forward, puzzling over the printed words.

"French," my father says, unwrapping the first package.

It's a letter opener. I lay it alongside Eric the Red's. Eric the Red's has a wavier blade, but my

father's designs are alive with peacocks and ser-
pents and curly-tailed monkeys.

He unwraps a soapstone Sphinx, a brass ash-
tray, and a five-link chain carved from a single
piece of wood. My mother and I lean forward
over the table, touching, exclaiming.

"And this," my father says, unwrapping the
last object.

He seems to be very pleased with himself.
He's smiling shyly. The paper falls away, revealing something carved from dark wood, something solid yet also slender, spidery, and airy.

"Know what it is?" he asks.

I say, "A church?"

"Chartres Cathedral," he says. "In France."

I reach out and touch my fingertips to the
finely carved arches, crosses, and soaring spires.

I pick it up.

The wood gleams where he held it a long time
ago. There are tiny burrs where his knife slipped.
I feel that I really am holding a crumbling stone
building in my hands.

We sit like that for a while, touching every-thing—my flute, his carvings.

Then he stands in his decisive way and packs everything away again.

As he's going out the door, he turns and points at Eric the Red's letter opener. "In the future, you be a bit more careful who you talk to, hear?"

It's almost the old voice and manner, but this time he can't quite keep the music out.